PRIDE AND PREJUDICE

JANE AUSTEN

www.realreads.co.uk

Retold by Gill Tavner
Illustrated by Ann Kronheimer

Published by Real Reads Ltd
Stroud, Gloucestershire, UK
www.realreads.co.uk

First published in 2008
Reprinted 2011

ISBN 978-1-906230-06-7

Printed in China by Wai Man Book Binding (China) Ltd
Designed by Lucy Guenot
Typeset by Bookcraft Ltd, Stroud, Gloucestershire

CONTENTS

THE CHARACTERS

Elizabeth Bennet

Elizabeth is lively, clever and proud of her ability to judge other people. Is she right to dislike Mr Darcy, or has she made a terrible mistake?

Jane Bennet

Jane, Elizabeth's elder sister, is beautiful, gentle, and in love. Will Mr Bingley ever offer her the happiness she deserves?

Mr Darcy

Wealthy and good-looking, Mr Darcy is surely a perfect husband for any young lady. Will he win Elizabeth's love, or will his pride always offend her?

Mr Bingley

Mr Bingley is handsome, rich and easy-going. Will he take Mr Darcy's advice, or follow his own heart in his search for happiness?

Lydia Bennet

Lydia is Jane and Elizabeth's younger sister. Will her foolish actions ruin the reputation and happiness of her entire family?

Mr Wickham

The gallant, charming Mr Wickham tells a sad story. Should Elizabeth believe him? Can *anybody* trust him?

Mr and Mrs Bennet

Mrs Bennet is desperate for her daughters to marry well, but her judgement is somewhat lacking. Will her long-suffering husband offer his family any guidance?

PRIDE AND PREJUDICE

THE PROPOSAL

Mr Darcy paced awkwardly around the room. Elizabeth, sitting and watching him, observed his fine, tall figure, and was surprised to sense uncertainty in his arrogant features. He sat down, cleared his throat as though to speak, said nothing, and stood up again. Why had this man, the last person in the world she wanted to see, come to disturb her peaceful evening?

Mr Darcy sat down again. 'It is no good,' he began, 'I have fought hard against my feelings, but it has been in vain. I must tell you how ardently I admire and love you. I should like you to be my wife.'

Elizabeth stared at him in astonishment, blushed, and remained silent.

Taking her silence as encouragement, Mr Darcy continued. 'Your mother is vulgar and embarrassing, your younger sister's behaviour is objectionable, and your father stubbornly fails to correct her. You and your elder sister somehow rise above your family with honour and good sense.' He smiled at Elizabeth. 'In spite of them all, you have earned my respect, admiration and love.' He awaited her grateful response.

Elizabeth struggled to control her voice. 'Mr Darcy, I cannot thank you for your proposal when you so freely offend me. You like me against your judgement and against your will. You will therefore be more relieved than disappointed by my refusal. Had you behaved in a more gentleman-like manner, I might at least have felt some compassion for you, but I do not.'

Mr Darcy stared in astonishment, but said nothing.

Elizabeth continued with feeling. 'I learned this afternoon that you were responsible for separating my dear sister Jane from your friend Mr Bingley, thus spoiling the happiness of two good people.'

Mr Darcy turned pale. 'Such a marriage would have brought shame to my friend. I have been kinder to him than I have been to myself.'

Now trembling, Elizabeth continued. 'Even if I had been able to overcome this scruple in my response to your proposal, I cannot forget your dishonourable treatment of poor Mr Wickham, whose life you have ruined.'

'Is this your opinion of me?' asked Mr Darcy, the quietness of his voice barely hiding his disappointment and anger.

'Yes. You are the last man in the world I would marry.'

Without another word Mr Darcy left the room. Watching from the window as his upright figure retreated along the garden path, Elizabeth was left in a terrible flutter. In spite of her dislike for him, it was flattering that the great Mr Darcy, one of the most eligible men in England, should love her.

They had parted in mutual disappointment, surprise and anger. It would be several hours before either was able to reflect dispassionately upon the events of the past few months. What could have led to Mr Darcy's extraordinary proposal? What had led to Elizabeth's firm rejection of his love?

BEFORE THE PROPOSAL

Like many mothers, Mrs Bennet was firmly of the belief that any single man in possession of a good fortune must be in want of a wife. As she had several daughters to dispose of, she was delighted to hear that such a gentleman was to move into the grand house at nearby Netherfield. 'What a fine thing this is for our girls,' she told her long-suffering husband.

Without lowering his newspaper, Mr Bennet rolled his eyes to the ceiling and sighed. His attempts to continue reading were in vain.

'I do so hope our new neighbour – he's called Mr Bingley, you know – will host a ball. I'm sure he will want to marry one of our girls.'

Mrs Bennet was anxious that her girls should all benefit from the security of wealthy husbands.

Mrs Bennet's wish for a ball was soon fulfilled. Invitations were received and promptly accepted, and several days of anticipation were endured before the great day finally arrived. The Bennet sisters looked beautiful, of course, and the gentlemen were all handsome.

Returning to her seat after an energetic dance, Elizabeth watched with pleasure as her sister Jane enjoyed her second dance with Mr Bingley. She smiled when she later overheard Mr Bingley tell his friend Mr Darcy that Jane was the most beautiful girl he had ever seen. 'Come, Darcy,' urged Mr Bingley, 'you have not yet graced the dance floor with your presence.'

'You know that I detest dancing unless I know my partner,' explained Mr Darcy, 'and there is not a woman in this room with whom it would be pleasant to dance.'

'Miss Elizabeth Bennet is sitting alone. She is very pretty. I will ask Jane to introduce you.'

Mr Darcy looked coldly at Elizabeth. Their eyes briefly met. 'She is quite pretty, but not pretty enough to tempt me.'

Elizabeth quickly decided that Mr Darcy was the proudest, most disagreeable man in the world. In the days following the ball, she discovered that other people shared her opinion.

Mr Bingley had been liked by everybody,
whereas Mr Darcy had given universal offence.
Elizabeth recounted the conversation she had
overheard with good humour. Her lively, playful
disposition enabled her to obtain enjoyment
from most situations, and she was happy to
laugh at herself.

Jane was modestly pleased to have received Mr Bingley's attentions. 'He is sensible and good humoured, with such perfect manners,' she told Elizabeth.

'He is also handsome,' teased her sister, 'as a gentleman should be.'

But Jane refused to condemn Mr Darcy's behaviour. She felt that he must have been misheard.

'Dear Jane, I have never heard you speak ill of anybody,' observed Elizabeth. 'Whatever you might say, I am determined to believe that Mr Darcy is arrogant and proud.'

Mr Darcy and Mr Bingley had been friends for many years. Each admired in the other the qualities that he himself lacked. Mr Bingley's manner was friendly and open, whilst Mr Darcy provided dignity and reliable judgement. Mr Darcy had been pleased when his friend invited him to spend a few weeks at Netherfield as part of a house party, which also included Bingley's sister Caroline.

After the ball, Mr Bingley eagerly told Darcy and his sister all about Jane.

'She smiles too much,' observed Mr Darcy.

Her curiosity aroused, Miss Bingley invited Jane to dine at Netherfield the following week.

As Mr Bennet's carriage was unavailable that day, Jane decided to ride to Netherfield, but before she was halfway there the skies opened and it started to pour with rain. Unfortunately, her soaking gave her a chill and she was unable to return home that  evening. The following morning, anxious about her sister, Elizabeth walked the three muddy miles to visit her at Netherfield.

Three miles of springing over puddles
left Elizabeth with a muddy hem and a face
glowing with health. When Elizabeth entered
the room, Mr Darcy's silent stare made her
feel uncomfortable. Far from meaning to be
rude, however, Mr Darcy was admiring the
beauty that exercise had given to their visitor's
complexion. What Elizabeth took for cold

contempt was in fact fascination with the spirit that sparkled in her eyes.

Miss Bingley, noticing Mr Darcy's admiring look, waited for her brother to lead Elizabeth upstairs to Jane's room. As soon as the door had closed behind them, she turned to Mr Darcy. 'I have never seen such bad manners and such ridiculous behaviour. She has six inches of mud on her petticoat and her hair looks almost wild. Don't you agree, Mr Darcy?'

'I was just thinking how much pleasure can be given by a pair of fine eyes in the face of a pretty woman.'

Miss Bingley fell silent.

Elizabeth nursed Jane at Netherfield for four more days. Mr Darcy found himself wishing to know more about Elizabeth. He was fascinated by her intelligent face, her beautiful brown eyes, and her easy, playful personality. He frequently found himself standing near to Elizabeth, enjoying her sparkling conversations with others.

'Don't you think I'm expressing myself remarkably well today, Mr Darcy?' teased Elizabeth on one such occasion.

'Yes, as always,' smiled Mr Darcy.

On the fourth day, when Jane was sufficiently recovered, Mr Bingley invited Mr and Mrs Bennet and their younger daughter Lydia to dine with them all at Netherfield. Mrs Bennet bustled in, bursting with admiration for the house. 'Oh, Mr Bingley, I do not know a place in the country that is equal to Netherfield ... ' She stopped suddenly when she caught sight of Mr Darcy. 'Oh Lizzie, that proud man is here,' she whispered.

Mr Darcy watched in horror and disbelief as, one by one, Elizabeth's family embarrassed themselves and everybody present. Lydia, only fifteen, spoke openly about her flirtations with the soldiers stationed in nearby Meryton. Far from stopping her, Mr Bennet smilingly confided in Mr Darcy, 'I do believe she is the silliest girl in England.' At the dinner table, Mrs Bennet whispered loudly to her husband, 'I am sure

Jane will soon be married to Mr Bingley.' Poor
Elizabeth, blushing with shame, wished her
mother would speak more quietly. Mr Darcy
looked across at his friend, who was deep in
conversation with Jane. Could Mrs Bennet be
right? Marriage into this family would surely
cause Mr Bingley a lifetime's embarrassment.
For himself too he felt that the evening provided
a useful warning. Were it not for Elizabeth's
undignified family, he too might have been in
danger of falling in love.

Amongst all the soldiers stationed at Meryton, one attracted more female admiration than any other. Mr Wickham was handsome and charming. Whatever he said, he said to please others; whatever he did, he did with gentlemanly grace. Elizabeth soon realised that she was the lucky girl towards whom his gallantry was principally directed.

One fine morning, as Mr Wickham accompanied Elizabeth and her sisters into town, their conversation was interrupted by the sound of an approaching horse. It was Mr Darcy, who dismounted to greet the group. He was cordial to the girls, but Elizabeth was surprised to see all friendliness drain from his face when he looked at Wickham.

Glancing at her soldier companion, she noticed that he had turned rather pale. After a few minutes of politeness, Mr Darcy rode away.

What could be the meaning of their strange reactions? Elizabeth was intrigued.

Fortunately she had to endure the suspense only until the following morning, when Mr Wickham introduced the topic she had half expected him to avoid. 'I was not aware that Darcy was in the area,' he began. 'Are you well acquainted with him?'

Elizabeth's delicacy abandoned her. 'More than I wish to be,' she replied. 'I find him disagreeable and proud.'

'You do not surprise me,' smiled Wickham.

'I have known his family all my life.' Noticing Elizabeth's astonishment, he continued. 'You were probably puzzled by the coldness of our meeting yesterday.'

Elizabeth nodded, awaiting an explanation.

'Darcy and I are not on friendly terms. My father worked for his father at Pemberley, their magnificent estate in Derbyshire. His father treated me as a second son. When the old gentleman died, he left money in his will to ensure my financial comfort, but his son prevented me from ever receiving the money.'

Elizabeth was shocked. Surely nobody could be so dishonourable as to pervert their own father's will.

'I had done nothing to deserve such treatment,' added Wickham. 'His only motive was jealousy of his father's affection towards me.'

'Then he deserves to be publicly disgraced,' observed Elizabeth indignantly. 'I can hardly believe him as bad as this. Surely his pride would prevent such dishonesty.'

'Oh, he is not entirely bad.' Mr Wickham retreated a little. 'He is generous to his tenants. To his young sister, he is a caring and affectionate brother. He is capable of being fair, sincere and agreeable. All of this, however, arises from his pride. His main motivation is to appear honourable.'

That evening Elizabeth repeated the conversation to Jane. Distressed by such a report, Jane could not believe Mr Darcy to be so bad.

'Dearest Jane,' smiled Elizabeth, 'you cannot think well of them both. Either Mr Darcy is guilty, or Mr Wickham is a liar. You must decide for yourself. I know what I think.'

'I cannot believe that Mr Bingley would be friends with such a man,' said Jane thoughtfully.

Another ball was about to take place, and Elizabeth prepared for it with uncharacteristic ill humour. Mr Wickham, with whom she had so hoped to dance, had decided not to attend.

'I wish to avoid a certain gentleman,' he explained. That certain gentleman was therefore much to blame for spoiling Elizabeth's evening before it had even begun.

Elizabeth's mood was not improved when Miss Caroline Bingley took a seat next to her as the music began. They watched as Jane and Mr Bingley opened the dancing. 'Don't you agree that my brother is capable of winning any lady's heart?' asked Miss Bingley.

Elizabeth smiled. He had certainly won Jane's.

'Of course, we all expect him to marry Mr Darcy's sister,' whispered Miss Bingley, as though confiding in an old friend. 'It is only a matter of time.'

Elizabeth's smile lost its warmth. 'Is your brother aware of this expectation?'

'Of course.'

'Then I wish him happiness in his attachment to such a family.'

Miss Bingley looked searchingly into Elizabeth's face. 'Ah,' she said, 'I see that Mr Wickham has been talking to you. I must warn you that Wickham is by no means a respectable man.'

'Thank you for your concern,' said Elizabeth coldly.

'You may of course ignore my warning if you wish,' sighed Miss Bingley, standing up. 'It was kindly meant.'

As the evening went on, Elizabeth noticed that Mr Darcy's eyes seemed to follow her wherever she went. She turned to find him standing beside her, awkward and silent. What could it mean? It could hardly be that he admired her. She decided to challenge him. 'Is there something amiss with my dress, Mr Darcy?'

'No, indeed,' Darcy replied. 'You look beautiful.'

Elizabeth felt flustered. When Mr Darcy asked for the pleasure of her company for the next dance, she quite forgot to refuse him.

They began the dance in silence.

'Well, Mr Darcy,' said his partner eventually. 'I see that we are both unsociable and unwilling to speak.'

'That may be true of me, Miss Bennet, but I cannot say that it is generally true of you.'

'I have been trying to work out your character,' she told him. 'I am puzzled by the different accounts that I have heard.'

'Do you consider yourself to be a good judge of character?' he asked.

'Excellent,' replied Elizabeth archly. 'I am rarely wrong.'

'And once your opinion is formed, do you allow yourself to be blinded by prejudice?'

'I hope not,' she smiled. 'Do you?'

'I am afraid I have faults,' said Mr Darcy, surprised to find himself speaking so openly, 'I am too unforgiving. My good opinion, once lost, is lost forever.'

An uncomfortable silence followed before Elizabeth felt able to venture what she really wanted to say. 'Mr Wickham has had the misfortune to lose your good opinion, for which he appears to be suffering.' Mr Darcy decided it was time to change the subject.

At that moment they were approached by an elderly gentleman. 'May I congratulate you upon your choice of partner, Mr Darcy? There is not a more beautiful girl in the room.'

Mr Darcy accepted the compliment with a gallant bow. The man continued, 'I hope to see you dance together again at your friend's forthcoming wedding.' Mr Darcy followed the man's eyes towards Bingley and Jane, who were once again dancing together.

For the rest of the evening, Darcy watched the happy couple studiously.

The next morning, Mr Darcy had much to think about. Watching Mr Bingley with Jane last night had assured him that his friend was indeed in love. However, Jane had behaved with such dignity and reserve that he had seen few signs to suggest that she felt the same. He was concerned for his friend.

Rather than feeling offended by Elizabeth's frank speaking, Darcy found her even more attractive. He wondered what Wickham had told her about him. Why was he to be constantly troubled by that man? Wickham had manipulated his father, and then squandered the money left to him in the will. When Mr Darcy had given him even more money, he had squandered that too. His greatest crime, however, had been his attempt to elope with

Mr Darcy's impressionable fifteen-year-old sister, Georgiana. Mr Darcy shuddered to remember the event. Fortunately, his sister had confided in him and the disaster was avoided. Now, Wickham had appeared in Meryton and seemed determined to turn everyone's opinion against Mr Darcy, including that of Elizabeth Bennet.

In order to free Bingley from Jane, and to save himself from Elizabeth's charms, Mr Darcy

decided to persuade Bingley to break up the house party, and leave Netherfield immediately. This would have the added benefit of removing himself from Wickham's painful presence.

Poor Mr Bingley, who had absolute respect for Mr Darcy's judgement and was naturally modest, was soon persuaded that he had misread Jane's friendliness, and that she was not in love with him. Mr Darcy's argument was eagerly supported by Miss Bingley, who was anxious to remove both men from the charms of the Bennet girls.

Within a week, Netherfield was empty.

The following weeks were most uncomfortable in the Bennet household. Mrs Bennet was inconsolable after the loss of Mr Bingley. 'My poor nerves are in tatters,' she complained.

In contrast to her mother, Jane struggled to hide her disappointment. 'I was mistaken to believe that he loved me,' she told Elizabeth. 'It was vanity on my side.' In spite of Jane's best efforts, her cheeks grew pale and thin. When her aunt, Mrs Gardiner, invited her to spend some time in London, everybody agreed that a change of scene would be beneficial.

Elizabeth was angered by her suspicion that Mr Bingley had been influenced by his friend and his sister. In addition to this, a cooling in Mr Wickham's attentions towards her offended her pride. His gallantry was now directed towards young Lydia, whose silly flirtation with him revealed the ease with which he could be flattered.

Above all else, Elizabeth missed Jane. With such a mother and such a foolish younger sister, her home was far from perfect. It was therefore with some relief that she accepted an invitation from her newly-married friend Charlotte to visit her in Kent. Elizabeth was interested to see Charlotte's new home and was also intrigued by the fact that she lived within the grounds of Lady Catherine de Bourgh's estate, Rosings.

As Lady Catherine was Darcy's aunt, Elizabeth was curious to learn more about her.

When she arrived in Kent, Elizabeth was greeted by Charlotte's husband. 'Miss Bennet, you have been afforded the greatest honour,' he enthused, helping her down from the coach.

'Lady Catherine has condescended to invite us all to dine with her at Rosings.' In case Elizabeth did not feel the honour quite as much as she ought, he described Rosings' grandeur in detail. 'Do not worry about your clothes,' he said, looking her up and down, 'her ladyship will not mind you being simply dressed. She likes to distinguish herself by her superior attire.' Elizabeth was amused to find Charlotte's husband so absurd.

Elizabeth's delight in absurd people was further gratified by Lady Catherine, who displayed even greater arrogance and pride than Mr Darcy himself. 'How old are you, Miss Bennet?' she asked rudely.

'You cannot expect me to own that,' smiled Elizabeth.

Lady Catherine decided that Elizabeth, one of the few people not to have treated her with anything other than grovelling subservience, was a rude, ill-bred girl.

'My nephew is to visit tomorrow,' announced Lady Catherine.

'Mr Darcy?' asked Elizabeth, slightly alarmed.

'Why, do you know him, Miss Bennet?'

Mr Darcy dutifully paid his annual visit to his aunt, accompanied by his good friend Colonel Fitzwilliam. Surprised to learn that Elizabeth was staying nearby, he persuaded Lady Catherine that it would be polite to invite her to dinner again.

When they had finished eating, Mr Darcy found himself watching Elizabeth as she moved across the room and sat down at the piano.

'Do you mean to frighten me, Mr Darcy, by listening to me play?' asked Elizabeth, as he walked towards her. 'I am not afraid of you, though I hear your sister plays so well.'

'Surely,' bowed Mr Darcy, 'you cannot truly believe that I have any intention of alarming you.'

The following morning, Mr Darcy visited Elizabeth at Charlotte's house. Pleased to find her alone, he accepted the chair she offered, and pulled it closer to hers. They sat and made awkward conversation. After a few minutes, he pulled his chair away again and left.

Mr Darcy's behaviour was most strange. A few days later, when Elizabeth told Charlotte about his visit, and told her how she kept bumping into him in the woods, Charlotte smiled. 'My dear Lizzie, he must be in love with you.'

Elizabeth found Colonel Fitzwilliam's company far more pleasant. He had the added attraction of being able to give her more information about Mr Darcy's character. 'He is a very caring brother to Miss Darcy,' he told her.

'He is also a loyal friend to me and to others. He recently told me that he had saved one of his friends from an embarrassing marriage. It seems that the lady showed little affection and her family little decency.'

Later, alone in her room, Elizabeth wept with anger and sorrow. Darcy's pride had ruined every hope of happiness for Jane. He had broken the most affectionate, most generous heart in the world.

Elizabeth's distress gave her a headache.

Rather than accompany Charlotte and her husband to Rosings that evening, she chose instead to sit alone and think about all that was bad about Mr Darcy.

It was most unfortunate for him that he chose that particular evening to knock on her door and make his proposal of marriage.

AFTER THE PROPOSAL

His proposal having been so rudely rejected by Elizabeth, Mr Darcy returned angrily to Rosings. He had not expected rejection, let alone insults. Her accusation of ungentleman-like behaviour stung him, and he could not forget the expression on Elizabeth's face when she said he was the last man in the world she would want to marry.

The following morning, he wrote Elizabeth a letter.

You last night accused me of two offences of a very different nature. The first was that I had detached Mr Bingley from your sister. I admit that I did indeed persuade my friend to leave Netherfield. I truly believed that Jane did not love him. Whilst I know now that I was mistaken, I also had other motives. In your heart, you must admit that your family cause you and your sister Jane pain by their indelicate behaviour.

The other accusation was that I had ruined the prospects of Mr Wickham. In fact Wickham did receive one thousand pounds from my father's will, and more besides from myself, all of which he has spent with great speed. In addition, it pains me to reveal that my sister, in her naivety, agreed to elope with Wickham. Had she not decided at the last minute to confide in me, she would have been ruined.

For the truth of everything here related, Colonel Fitzwilliam can vouch. I will only add, god bless you.

With the letter in his hand, he set off in the hope of meeting Elizabeth on one of her daily walks.

Elizabeth caught sight of Mr Darcy too late to avoid him.

'I hoped to meet you,' he said. 'Please do me the honour of reading this letter.' He bowed and walked away.

Sitting on a fallen tree trunk, Elizabeth, trembling, read the letter. With some pain, she had to admit his point about her family. When she read what he had written about Mr Wickham she cried out loud. 'Oh, I am ashamed of myself! How despicably I have acted!' She remembered how her vanity had been flattered by Wickham, and her pride offended by Darcy. It was upon this that she had based all her opinions. 'I have been blind and prejudiced! Until this moment, I never knew myself.'

Mr Darcy left Rosings the following day. Elizabeth thought it unlikely that their paths would cross again, and regretted that she would have no chance of apologising to Darcy for her prejudiced views of his character and behaviour.

Later that summer, Elizabeth accepted an invitation to travel in Derbyshire with her aunt. When her aunt suggested that they take the opportunity to visit Mr Darcy's nearby Pemberley estate, one of the most beautiful stately homes in England, Elizabeth's curiosity conflicted with her sense that such a visit would be inappropriate.

Her curiosity won.

Mr Darcy always enjoyed his summers at Pemberley. It had been home to him and his sister Georgiana all his life.

Enjoying a walk in the grounds one fine morning, he stopped dead in his tracks. Ahead of him was Elizabeth Bennet. Their eyes met, and the faces of both were instantly overspread with the deepest blush. It was a most uncomfortable moment. The first to recover, Mr Darcy greeted Elizabeth with his usual civility.

Elizabeth's embarrassment at being found at Pemberley was obvious. Mr Darcy decided that this was his opportunity to show Elizabeth how mistaken she had been about his character.

During the following week, Mr Darcy showed Elizabeth and her aunt warm hospitality. With understandable pride, he showed them around his home and introduced them to Georgiana.

Miss Darcy later told her brother how much she liked Elizabeth, and gently hinted to him that she would be a very welcome addition to the family at Pemberley. Mr Darcy was very pleased.

At the end of the week, when Elizabeth left Derbyshire to return home, Mr Darcy decided that it might be a good idea to visit Mr Bingley and persuade him to return to Netherfield immediately.

As Darcy had anticipated, Bingley was easily persuaded.

Though she had been mortified to be discovered at Pemberley, Elizabeth was most grateful for Mr Darcy's sensitive and generous hospitality. She was flattered by his attentions to her, and delighted by Pemberley itself. Though she was afraid even to consider that he might still be in love with her after her terrible treatment of him, she could not help reflecting that it might be rather pleasant to be mistress of Pemberley. She left Derbyshire with a confused heart.

Even greater confusion awaited her when she arrived home. Her mother, in tears of violent grief, flew into her arms. 'Oh Lizzie, Lydia has gone! Oh, what a terrible man! I know he will not marry her. Mr Bennet must go after them. He will have to fight a duel.'

Turning to Jane for a sensible explanation of what had happened, Elizabeth learned that they had just received news that Lydia had run away with a soldier from Meryton.

'Who is the man?' asked Elizabeth, dreading the answer.

'Mr Wickham.'

Elizabeth sat down. There might not be much sense in her mother's words, but she was right about one thing. From what Elizabeth now knew about Wickham's character, she was certain that he would not marry Lydia. Elizabeth angrily reflected that Lydia's foolish action had damaged far more than just herself. She had brought misery and humiliation upon them all. What gentleman would now associate himself with such a family? Not Mr Bingley, and certainly not Mr Darcy.

After two days of trying to calm her mother while they tried to find out where Lydia had gone, Elizabeth was very tired. A knock on the door made it necessary that she compose herself. When the door opened, however, Elizabeth's astonishment at seeing Mr Darcy standing there took away all that composure. She burst into tears.

'Good god, what is the matter?' asked Mr Darcy, gently supporting her as they went back inside.

'Lydia has eloped with Mr Wickham,' sobbed Elizabeth.

'I am grieved indeed,' said Mr Darcy, frowning. He became thoughtful and gloomy. Elizabeth watched with sadness. Her attractiveness was surely fading in his eyes. All hope now lost, she realised how much she cared for him.

Mr Darcy had felt nervous about visiting Elizabeth's home. Would she be angry or pleased that he had followed her all the way from Pemberley? Did her friendliness last week mean that she might reconsider his proposal?

As soon as she opened the door and told him about Wickham, his plans changed. That evening, he left a surprised Mr Bingley alone at Netherfield and headed for London.

Two days later, Mr Darcy traced Wickham to a London inn and confronted him with his misdeed.

'How much will it take to make you honour Miss Lydia Bennet?' he asked the grinning soldier.

'Enough to cover my gambling debts would be a good beginning.'

Mr Darcy nodded. He felt embarrassed by Wickham's lack of dignity and integrity.

'I will also need enough to support myself and Lydia for a year,' continued Wickham, 'should I agree to marry her,' he added slyly.

Mr Darcy nodded again. 'I will give you half of the money now, and half after your wedding. I insist, however, that nobody should ever discover that I have given you this money.'

'Why are you involving yourself?'

'I feel responsible. Had I not been too proud to tell people about your low character, they would not have trusted you. Furthermore, as I suspect that your action is designed to gain more money from me, I am further responsible for the Bennets' unhappiness, and am forced to help.'

'Is there not another reason?' Wickham smiled.

Mr Darcy did not answer. Certainly, if Lydia married Wickham her family's respectability and, more specifically, that of her sisters, would be restored.

In the midst of all the anxiety, Elizabeth had to face another, most unexpected, trial. Lady Catherine de Bourgh had condescended to travel all the way from Rosings to pay her a visit.

The grand lady looked haughtily around Elizabeth's home. 'A modest house displaying little taste,' she observed. 'Still, who could expect

taste from such a
family as yours?
I have heard about
your sister's recent
behaviour.'

With difficulty,
Elizabeth remained
silent.

Lady Catherine
chose a seat. 'You
know why I am here, don't you?'

Elizabeth didn't.

'I think you have charmed my nephew.
However, you must promise not to get engaged to
him.'

Astonished by her rudeness, Elizabeth answered,
'I will make no such promise.'

'Any connection with your family will disgrace
him.'

'I am a gentleman's daughter, and Mr Darcy is a
gentleman. If I am his choice, why may I not accept?'

'You obstinate, headstrong girl,' said Lady Catherine as she marched from the house, leaving Elizabeth in a flutter of anger and astonishment. What a dreadful woman she was!

A few days later a letter arrived from Lydia. 'I can barely write for laughing!' she wrote. 'My Wickham and I are married. How jolly to be married before my sisters. That proud Mr Darcy was at our wedding ... oh, I promised not to mention his name ... my dear Wickham will be quite cross ... '

Elizabeth quickly read the rest of Lydia's letter. Why had Mr Darcy been at Lydia's wedding? How had Wickham been persuaded to do the honourable thing and marry her? A reference later in the letter to Wickham's suddenly receiving a considerable sum of money caught her attention. She sat. She thought. She wondered.

Could it possibly be that Mr Darcy had saved Lydia and all of her family from disgrace?

Could it possibly be that he deserved all the gratitude in the world?

As Lady Catherine stood before him, reporting Elizabeth's outrageous responses to her demands, Mr Darcy reflected to himself that he had been wrong about many things.

Jane did love Mr Bingley, and a person should not always be judged by their family. He certainly hoped that Elizabeth would not judge him by his aunt. He could not help smiling. Elizabeth's refusal to promise his aunt not to marry him gave him hope.

The following morning, Mr Darcy and Mr Bingley rode to the Bennets' home. After a meeting with a stunned Mr Bennet in his study, each went to find their chosen sister.

Mr Darcy found Elizabeth reading. She stood

up quickly, eager to thank him. He stopped her. 'Elizabeth, if your feelings are still as they were at Rosings, please tell me. *My* affections and wishes are unchanged.'

Feeling happiness beyond anything she had felt before, Elizabeth assured him that her feelings were now entirely different. They spent the next few hours walking, and talking about all that had happened between them, each admitting their own errors.

'I was indeed too proud,' confessed Mr Darcy.

'And I was too prejudiced,' laughed Elizabeth.

They found Jane and Mr Bingley holding hands in the parlour. 'Oh Lizzy, how shall I bear such happiness?' asked Jane. 'Why is everybody not as happy as I am?' She stopped and looked quizzically at Elizabeth's smiling face.

'I am sorry to tell you, dear Jane, that it is already decided between Mr Darcy and I that *we* are to be the happiest couple in the world.'

Mr and Mrs Bennet walked in. Mr Bennet

warmly congratulated both gentlemen. For a rare moment Mrs Bennet was silent, then her emotions overcame her, 'Good gracious! Bless me! Three daughters married! Mr Darcy and Mr Bingley! Girls, didn't I always say that every single man in possession of a fortune must be in want of a wife?'

TAKING THINGS FURTHER

The real read

This *Real Read* version of *Pride and Prejudice* is a retelling of Jane Austen's magnificent work. If you would like to read the full novel in all its original splendour, many complete editions are available, from bargain paperbacks to beautifully-bound hardbacks. You may well find a copy in your local charity shop.

Filling in the spaces

The loss of so many of Jane Austen's original words is a sad but necessary part of the shortening process. We have had to make some difficult decisions, omitting subplots and details, some important, some less so, but all interesting. We have also, at times, taken the liberty of combining two events into one, or of giving a character words or actions that originally belong to another. The points below will fill in some of the gaps, but nothing can beat the original.

- In this *Real Reads* version of *Pride and Prejudice*, we have changed the order in which the story is told. Jane Austen tells the story in the order in which events happen, and so Mr Darcy's proposal is in the middle of the book.

- Jane Austen only tells us the truth about Mr Wickham, in Mr Darcy's letter, after the proposal.

- Mr and Mrs Bennet actually have two more daughters. Kitty is similar to Lydia, whereas Mary is very serious and tends to moralise.

- Because he has no son, Mr Bennet's estate will eventually be inherited by a male cousin, Mr Collins, rather than by his daughters. Mrs Bennet is therefore understandably anxious for her daughters to marry well before she and Mr Bennet die.

- Mr Collins is a foolish clergyman. He offers to marry Elizabeth, who refuses. Soon after, he proposes to Elizabeth's friend, Charlotte Lucas.

Having no other prospect of marriage, Charlotte accepts. Charlotte and Mr Collins are the friends Elizabeth visits near to the home of Lady Catherine de Bourgh.

● Lady Catherine de Bourgh expects that Mr Darcy will marry her daughter, Anne. This helps to explain her opposition to his marrying Elizabeth.

● The aunt that Elizabeth travels with to Derbyshire is called Mrs Gardiner; she and her husband, Elizabeth's uncle, are very sensible people. They had offered to take Elizabeth to the Lake District, but had to cancel and decided instead that Elizabeth and her aunt should travel in Derbyshire. When they visit Pemberley, they have been assured that Mr Darcy is away from home. Had she known that he would be there, Elizabeth would not have agreed to visit.

- Mr Darcy's housekeeper speaks very warmly of her master. This is when Elizabeth begins to consider that her own opinion of him might be wrong.

- The story of Wickham and Lydia's elopement is more complex in the original version than in this *Real Read*.

Back in time

Pride and Prejudice is probably Jane Austen's most well-known and most popular novel, thanks to its sparkling wit, enduring subject matter and romantic plot.

In Jane Austen's time, the relationship between marriage and money was very important. Women were neither expected nor educated to work for a living. Furthermore, estates were usually inherited by the eldest son. If there was no son, they would be left to the nearest male relative. This is why Mr Bennet's estate will pass to Mr Collins.

Marrying a wealthy man was, for many women, the most respectable way to gain independence and achieve comfort.

The moral code governing relations between men and women was very strict. Lydia's flirting with the soldiers is inappropriate. By eloping with Wickham she could ruin her own reputation and respectability as well as that of her family. It is only through Mr Darcy's actions in making Wickham marry Lydia that the Bennet family's social standing is saved.

Jane Austen was writing at a time of major change. Although she would have been aware of the violent social conflicts of her time, she chose to concentrate on the minute details of everyday life. She once described her writing as 'this little bit of ivory upon which I work with so fine a brush to produce litle effect after much labour'. Her 'little bit of ivory' is human interaction, as fascinating today as it was to her. Thanks to Jane's talent, Mr Darcy still makes female hearts beat a little faster.

Finding out more

We recommend the following books and websites to gain a greater understanding of Jane Austen's England:

Books

- Gill Hornby, *Who was Jane Austen? The Girl with the Magic Pen*, Short Books, 2005.

- Jon Spence, *Becoming Jane Austen*, Hambledon Continuum, 2007.

- Josephine Ross, *Jane Austen's Guide to Good Manners: Compliments, Charades and Horrible Blunders*, Bloomsbury, 2006.

- Dominique Enwright, *The Wicked Wit of Jane Austen*, Michael O'Mara, 2007.

- Lauren Henderson, *Jane Austen's Guide to Romance: The Regency Rules*, Headline, 2007.

- Deirdre Le Faye, *Jane Austen: The World of Her Novels*, Frances Lincoln, 2003.

- Brenda Sneathen Mattox, *Pride and Prejudice Paper Dolls*, Dover, 2000.

Websites

- www.janeausten.co.uk
Home of the Jane Austen Centre in Bath, England.

- www.janeaustensoci.freeuk.com
Home of the Jane Austen Society. Includes summaries of, and brief commentary on, her novels.

- www.bbc.co.uk/drama/prideandprejudice
Accessible information about the book, along with photographs and clips from the highly successful TV drama.

- www.pemberley.com
A very enthusiastic site for Jane Austen enthusiasts.

- www.literaryhistory.com/19thC/AUSTEN
A selective and helpful guide to links to other Jane Austen sites.

Film

- *Pride and Prejudice* (1995), adapted by Andrew Davies, BBC Films.

Food for thought

Here are some things to think about if you are reading *Pride and Prejudice* alone, or ideas for discussion if you are reading it with friends.

In retelling *Pride and Prejudice* we have tried to recreate, as accurately as possible, Jane Austen's original plot and characters. We have also tried to imitate aspects of her style. Remember, however, that this is not the original work; thinking about the points below, therefore, can help you begin to understand Jane Austen's craft. To move forward from here, turn to the full-length version of *Pride and Prejudice* and lose yourself in her wonderful portrayals of human nature.

Starting points

● Which character interests you the most? Why?

● Do you have more sympathy for Elizabeth or Mr Darcy? Why? Did your feelings change as you read the book?

● How did your feelings about Mr Wickham change while you read the book?

● What do you think about Miss Bingley?

● Look up 'pride' and 'prejudice' in a dictionary. See if you can find examples of characters' actions resulting from their pride or prejudice.

● Which character do you think learns the most? What does he or she learn?

Themes

What do you think Jane Austen is saying about the following themes in *Pride and Prejudice*?

- pride

- prejudice

- love and marriage

- politeness and good manners

- choices for young women

Style

Can you find paragraphs containing examples of the following?

- a person exposing their true character through something they say

- humour

- gentle irony, where the writer makes the reader think one thing whilst saying something different; this is often a way of gently mocking one of the characters

Look closely at how these paragraphs are written. What do you notice? Can you write a paragraph in the same style?